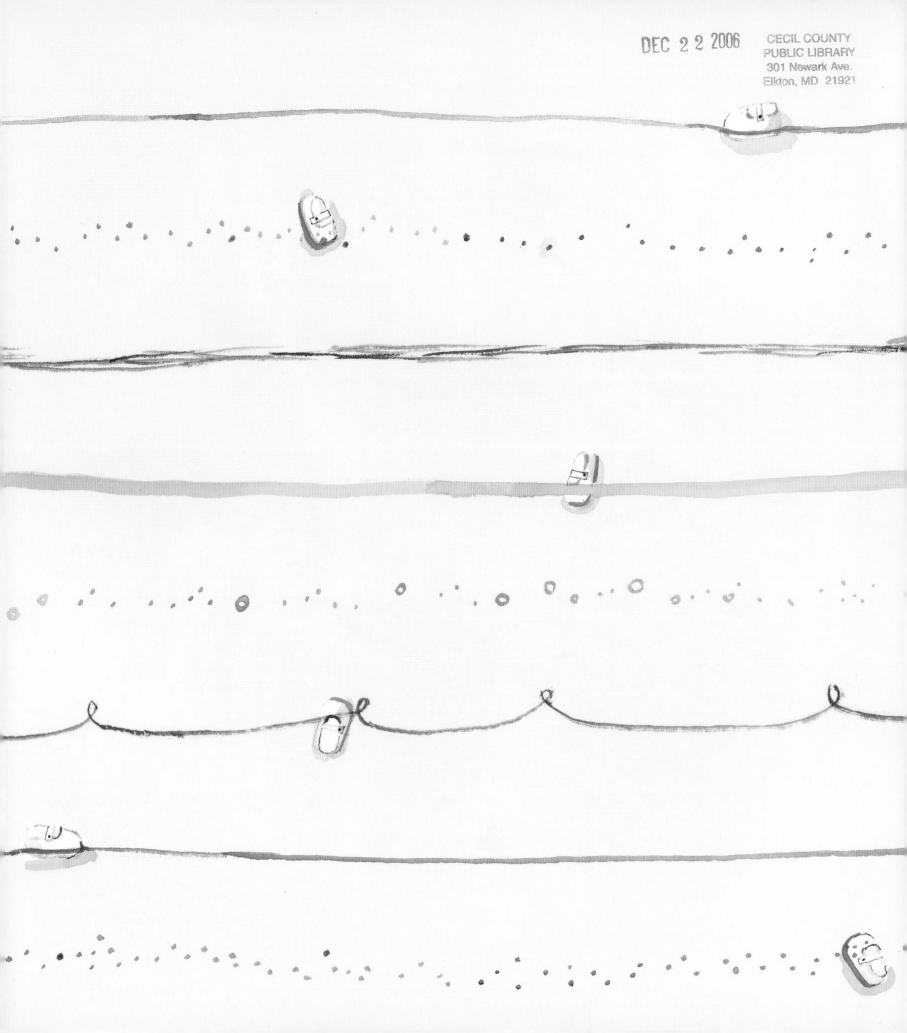

Baby Shoes

by **Dashka Slater**
pictures by **Hiroe Nakata**

BLOOMSBURY
CHILDREN'S
BOOKS

For Cliff, with all my love. — D.S.

To my little bump. — H.N.

Text copyright © 2006 by Dashka Slater
illustrations copyright © 2006 by Hiroe Nakata

Typeset in Klepto
Art created with watercolors
Book design by Teresa K. Dikun
Published by Bloomsbury Publishing, New York, London, and Berlin
Distributed to the trade by Holtzbrinck Publishers

Library of Congress Cataloging-in-Publication Data
Slater, Dashka.
Baby shoes / Dashka Slater ; pictures by Hiroe Nakata.—1st U.S. ed.
p.   cm.
Summary: After taking a walk with his mother, Baby's new white shoes
with the blue stripe are covered with a variety of colors.
iSBN-10: 1-58234-684-4 • iSBN-13: 978-1-58234-684-7
[1. Shoes—Fiction. 2. Color—Fiction. 3. Stories in rhyme.] i. Nakata, Hiroe, ill. ii. Title.
PZ8.3.S63Bab 2006   [E]—dc22   2005053581

First U.S. Edition 2006
Printed in China
1 3 5 7 9 10 8 6 4 2

Bloomsbury Publishing, Children's Books, U.S.A.
175 Fifth Avenue, New York, NY 10010

Baby's got some brand-new shoes,
white as light, stripe of blue.
He passed over all the rest,
chose the ones he liked the best.

White shoes.
High-jumping,
fast-running,
fine-looking
shoes!

Mama and Baby take a walk.
Baby brings some colored chalk.

Uses red to draw a rose

and some red loops on the toes

of those white,
high-jumping,
fast-running,
loop-de-looping
shoes!

Baby says, "Uh - oh!"

Mama says, "Oh, no!"

But those shoes just go, go, go.

Baby likes to run so fast,
spins in circles on the grass.
After all those jumps and hops . . .

...guess what has green polka dots?

Those white, high-jumping, fast-running, dizzy-spinning **shoes!**

Baby says,
"Uh - oh!"

Mama says,
"Oh, no!"

But those shoes just go, go, go.

From the big tree dropping down
plums go SPLAT and hit the ground.
Baby stops to take a peek . . .

...gives those shoes a purple streak.
Those white,
high-jumping,
fast-running,
fruit-kicking
shoes!

Baby says, "Uh-oh!"

Mama says,

"Oh, no!"

But those shoes just go, go, go.

City workers painting signs
touch up yellow crosswalk lines.
Baby hops across the street . . .

...gets some yellow on his feet.
On those white,
high-jumping, fast-running,
can't-miss-'em **shoes!**

Baby says,
"Uh-oh!"

Mama says,
"Oh, no!"

But those shoes just go, go, go.

Baby finds a puddle deep,
takes a bouncing, hopping leap.
After splashing round and round . . .

. . . Baby's shoes have rings of brown.

Those white,
high-jumping,
fast-running,
splish-splashing
shoes!

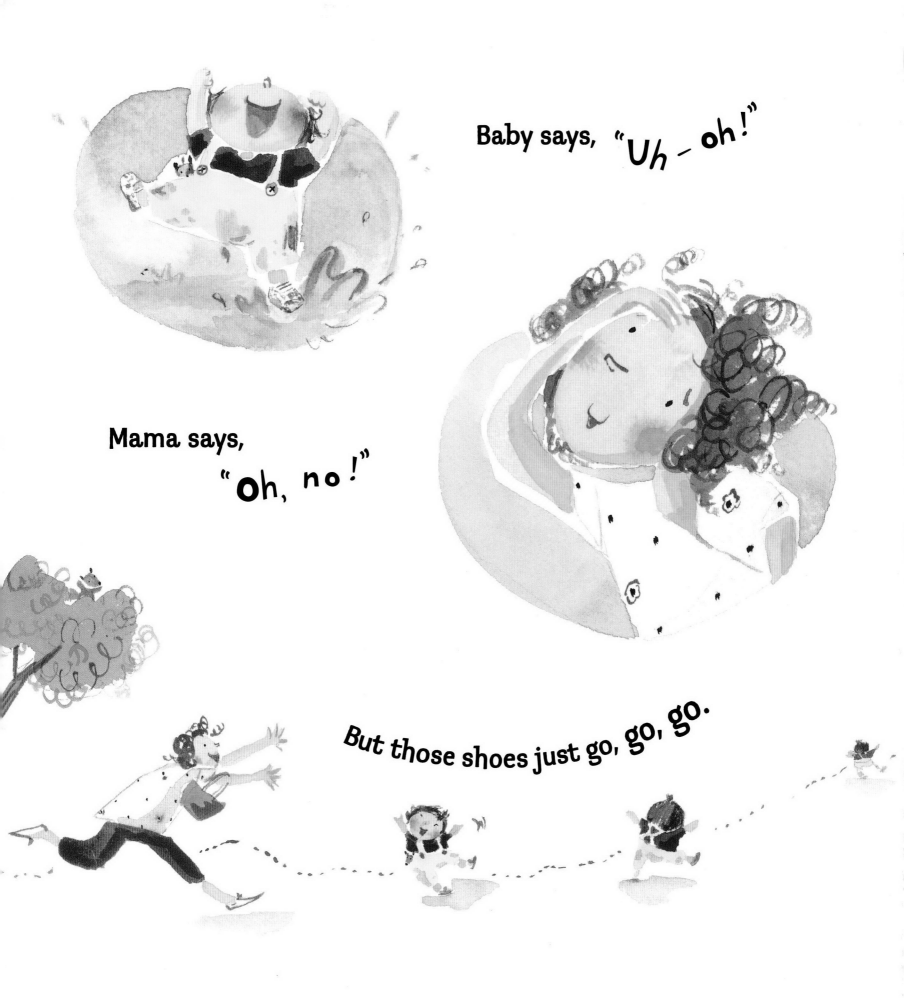

Baby says, "Uh-oh!"

Mama says, "Oh, no!"

But those shoes just go, go, go.

Baby's got some brand-new shoes,
colored bright in many hues.
Doesn't matter **what** folks say—
Baby likes them best that way.

Those
speckled, spotted,
polka-dotted,
puddle-stomping,
rainbow-romping,

go-go-going shoes.